Bob the **Builder**™

Spud The Dragon

Bob's Boots

Pilchard Goes Fishing

Bob's Big Surprise

CD Story Book

HINKLER
BOOKS

CD Story Book

Spud the Dragon

•

Bob's Boots

•

Bob's Big Surprise

•

Pilchard Goes Fishing

Hinkler Books Pty Ltd
17-23 Redwood Drive
Dingley, VIC 3172 Australia
www.hinklerbooks.com
Reprinted 2004(twice)

© 2003 HIT Entertainment PLC and Keith Chapman.
All rights reserved. Bob the Builder and all related logos and characters are trademarks of
HIT entertainment PLC and Keith Chapman.

Spud the Dragon – First published in the UK in 1999 by BBC Worldwide, Ltd.
Bob's Boots – First published in the UK in 1998 by BBC Worldwide, Ltd.
Bob's Big Surprise – First published in the UK in 1999 by BBC Worldwide, Ltd.
Pilchard Goes Fishing – First published in the UK in 1998 by BBC Worldwide, Ltd.
US edition published in 2002 by Simon Spotlight.

This edition published in 2003 by Hinkler Books Pty Ltd.
With thanks to HOT Animation.

ISBN: 1 7412 1082 8

Printed and bound in China

CONTENTS

Bob the Builder™

Spud the Dragon

HINKLER BOOKS

One morning, Wendy and Bob started loading strange pink rolls onto Muck's digger.

"What's this stuff, Bob?" asked Muck.

"It's insulation, Muck," said Bob. "Wendy and I are going to put it in Mrs. Potts' attic. It saves energy by stopping heat escaping through the roof!"

"It's like a winter hat for a house!" laughed Dizzy.

"I think that's everything," said Bob.

"Can you fix it?" called Scoop.

"Yes we can!!" the others shouted.

"Yeah ... I think so," muttered Lofty.

Meanwhile, in the schoolyard, Mrs. Percival was sorting out a pile of costumes and props. Spud arrived with a ladder.

"Hello, Mrs. Percival!" called Spud. "Here's the ladder you wanted to borrow from Farmer Pickles!"

"Oh! Thanks," said Mrs. Percival. "I need it for the school play tonight." She waved goodbye as she took the ladder inside.

Spud noticed a pirate's costume among the props. He couldn't resist trying it on.

"Ha har ha haa! Long John Spud!" said Spud the Pirate. "Fiercest pirate of the seven seas!"

Next, Spud saw a cowboy hat and a hobby horse.

"Hi ho Spud, away!" cried Spud the Cowboy. "The lone scarecrow rides again!"

He galloped around the yard and saw a package of paint.

"Face paint! A scarecrow could have a lot of fun with that!" said Spud in delight, as he grabbed the face paint. Then Spud noticed a dragon costume and crawled inside.

"I'm Spud the Dragon! Roarrrrrrr!!!" he growled. "Mrs. Percival won't mind if I borrow this, and I'll bring it back in time for the school play."

And Spud the Dragon crept out of the schoolyard to make some mischief.

At Mrs. Potts' house, Wendy and Bob were in the attic laying the insulation. The attic was full of old boxes of material, colorful banners and old curtains.

"I'm afraid there's lots of old junk up there!" called Mrs. Potts. "You never know when something might come in handy!"

"What's this?" said Bob, rummaging in the boxes.

"A tambourine!"

Bob danced around the boxes of colorful junk in the attic.

Meanwhile, Spud the Dragon saw Muck going back to the yard.

"Hello there Muck," said Spud. "I'm a magic dragon!"

"M-m-magic d-dragon!" quivered Muck. "How do you know my name?"

"I'm magic," said Spud. "Bla ... I know everything! Would you like me to grant you a wish?"

"Yes please!" cried Muck.

"OK, close your eyes," said Spud.

"Oh," Muck pondered possible wishes. "I know! I wish I had a great big pile of mud to play around in!"

Meanwhile, while Muck's eyes were closed, Spud drew a cat's face on Muck with the face paint.

When Muck's eyes opened, the magic dragon was gone!

"He's disappeared!" whispered Muck. "He was really magic. But, where's my wish? Maybe it's waiting for me back at the yard."

When Muck trundled into the yard the machines began to laugh.

"Oh, hello Muck!" said Roley.

"What do you have on your face, Muck?" giggled Dizzy.

"What? Is it, is it mud?" asked Muck.

"No! You've got a cat face!" cried Scoop.

"Wow! I wonder if it has anything to do with the magic dragon?" mused Muck.

Spud the Dragon was still on the loose.
"Ha ha! Here comes Lofty! This will be fun!"
he laughed.

As Lofty trundled past,
Spud leapt into the road.
"Roarrrrrr!!!"
he shouted. "I'm a scary
fire-breathing dragon ..."
"Oooh!" trembled Lofty.
"... with googly eyes!"
added Spud.
"Aaaarrrrghhhh!"
squealed Lofty, and raced
off to tell Bob and
Wendy.
"Ha ha!" laughed
Spud. "Spud the Dragon
strikes again!"

When he got to the site, Lofty was terrified.

"Bob! Wendy!" he cried. "A big fierce dragon really scared me!"

"Oh Lofty. There aren't any dragons around here," said Wendy.

"There are, I saw one!" replied Lofty. "It had … er … googly eyes!"

"Now come on. It's all right," said Wendy. "Tell you what, I'll ride back to the yard with you to make sure that there are no dragons around."

Together they headed back to the yard.

"Hi everybody!" called Wendy when they arrived.

"Wendy! Look!" cried Scoop.

"A magic dragon painted on my face!" said Muck.

"Oh! I saw a dragon too!" quivered Lofty.

"Hmmmm," pondered Wendy. "Sounds to me like someone's being naughty!"

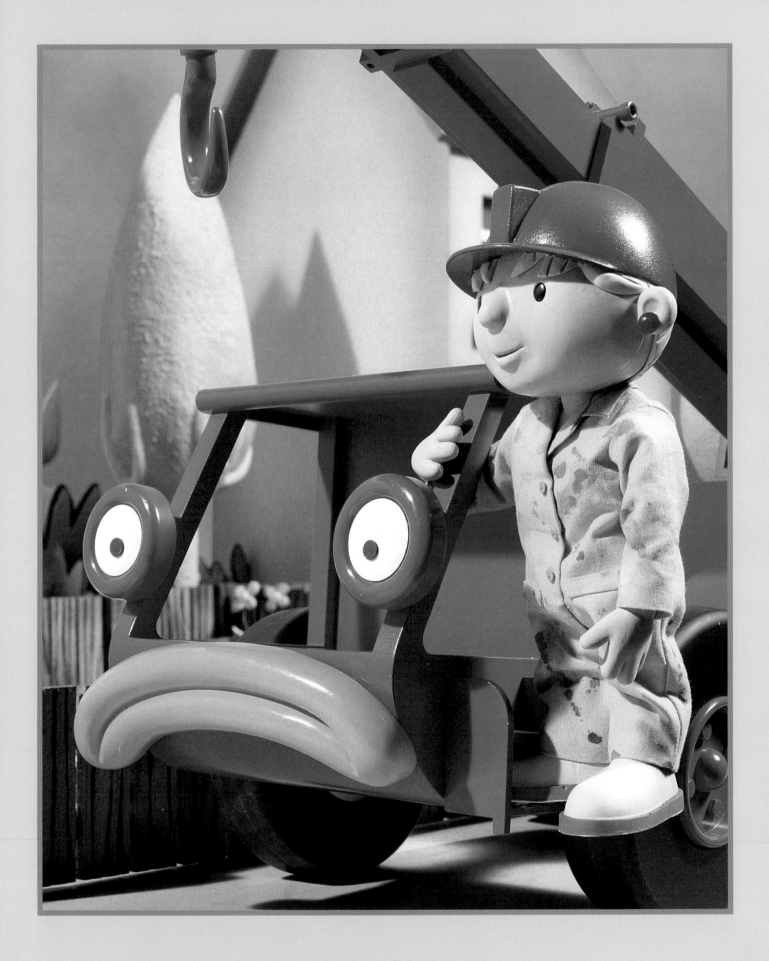

Wendy, Muck and Lofty went back to the site to help Bob finish the insulation. Soon Bob was dusting off his hands after a job well done.

"Oh, thanks Bob! Thanks Wendy!" cried Mrs. Potts.

They were all heading home when suddenly, from out of the bushes, a dragon appeared on the road!

"**Roarrrrr!!!**" shouted the dragon.

"Oh! It's the scary dragon!" trembled Lofty.

"It's the magic dragon!" cried Muck.

"It's not a dragon at all," said Wendy suspiciously. "I know that voice!"

"Uh oh!" said the dragon. He leapt over the wall and raced off into the forest.

"Come on—let's get him!" shouted Bob.

Wendy and Bob chased the dragon through the trees.

"Woaaahhhhh!" cried the dragon, as he tripped over his costume and fell into a puddle of mud. Wendy and Bob soon caught up.

"Ha ha! I thought so!" cried Wendy. "Spud the Dragon!"

"I'm sorry, Wendy," said Spud miserably. "I was just having some fun with Mrs. Percival's costume."

"Look at it, Spud. It's ruined!" said Bob.

"I think we'd better go and tell Mrs. Percival what happened," said Wendy.

"Oh no!" cried Mrs. Percival, when she saw the damaged costume. "I don't know if we can fix this in time for tonight!"

"I'm really sorry, Mrs. Percival," said Spud sadly.

"Just a minute, I have an idea," said Wendy, as she walked out of the schoolyard.

The others wondered what she could be planning. Half an hour later, the dragon appeared again in the schoolyard!

"Ta da!" said Wendy, as she pulled off the dragon head. "One dragon costume!"

"It's fantastic, Wendy!" said Mrs. Percival.

"You used Mrs. Potts' old junk," said Bob. "It's Wendy the Dragon now!"

Wendy put the dragon head back on. Just then, Spud saw the dragon.

"Roarrrrrrrr!" cried Wendy the Dragon.

"Aaaarrghhhh!" squealed Spud, as he ran off down the road.

The End

HINKLER BOOKS

O ne morning a big, brown parcel arrived for Bob. He showed it to Finn.

"Look what came in the mail, Finn," said Bob. "My new boots! What do you think Finn?"

Finn did a back flip in his tank to show how much he liked Bob's new boots. Bob was excited.

"You know, I think I'll wear them to work today," said Bob.

In the yard, Wendy was telling everyone their jobs for the day.

"Er … Lofty you're with Bob today," said Wendy. "He needs you to help fix a broken gate."

Bob rushed out to show them all his new boots. When he walked around, there was a squeaking noise.

"Shhh everyone," said Bob. "I can hear squeaking."

When Bob stopped walking, the squeaking stopped too.

"Uh, I can't hear anything," whispered Muck.

When Bob started walking again, the squeaking noise came back.

"Oh yes, I can hear it now," said Wendy.

"Ha ha! It sounds like mice!" laughed Dizzy.

"OHHHHH," trembled Lofty. "MmmMMICE!"

"Don't worry Lofty. It's not mice," said Wendy.

"Ohh … Oh if … if you're sure," said Lofty, who was frightened of mice.

But they could all hear the squeaking noise when Bob walked around the yard.

"Ha ha ha, Bob I know where the squeaks are coming from," laughed Wendy.

"Where?" asked Bob.

"Your new boots," said Wendy. "They need to be broken in to soften the leather."

"Ha ha! You sound like you need oiling, Bob," Scoop laughed.

"Well, we'd better get some work done," said Bob.

"Can we fix it?" called Scoop.

"YES WE CAN!!!" everyone shouted.

Meanwhile, Spud, Travis and Farmer Pickles were trying to work out the best way to get to Bob's yard.

"… You see, Travis," said Spud, "the quickest way to Bob's yard is to go left at the fork."

"I'm sure it's right," disagreed Travis.

Bird, who was watching them talking, was starting to get confused.

"Oh well now," said Farmer Pickles. "They say the quickest way is usually as the crow flies. It means the quickest way to get to anywhere is in a straight line."

"I can walk faster than any old bird can fly," said Spud. "Bird, come on, I'll race you to Bob's yard."

Later, on their job, Bob and Lofty tried to lower the gate into place, but a strong wind was blowing it around.

"Left a little. OK ... straight down," said Bob. "That's it, Lofty. Phew! I think it must be time for lunch."

"Ooh, what have you got today, Bob?" asked Lofty.

"My favorite," said Bob happily. "Peanut butter and jelly sandwiches and a big cream puff."

When Bob opened his lunchbox, a gust of wind picked up his napkin.

"Quick Lofty," cried Bob. "It's blowing away!"

They both raced off to catch the napkin. Bob's new boots squeaked noisily with each step.

Just then Bird flew by, with Spud right behind him.

"Huh, oh, oh I'm tired!" said Spud. "Ah … and hungry!"

Bob's lunchbox was open on the ground, but Bob and Lofty were nowhere to be seen.

"Wow, I wonder whose lunch this is," said Spud. "Well, hee hee Finders Keepers. Ha ha!"

Spud took a bite of one of Bob's sandwiches.

"Urrgh, peanut butter and jelly!" frowned Spud, but then he saw Bob's cream puff.

"Ah what's this," said Spud "Hey! A cream puff!"

Suddenly Spud noticed that Bird was getting away.

"Hey, wait for me, Bird!" called Spud, putting the cream puff in his pocket. "I'm going to save this till I get to the yard … mmm!"

Bob and Lofty chased the napkin into a field where three little mice lived. The mice heard Bob's boots squeaking and started to follow him.

"Squeak squeak squeak!" said Bob's boots.

"Eek eek eek!" said the mice.

Finally Bob caught the napkin.

"Ooh, phew," said Bob. "Got it Lofty. Ah, I'm ready for my lunch, after all that running around."

They headed back to Bob's lunchbox, but it was empty.

"Hold it, who's been eating my sandwiches?" cried Bob. "Where's my cream puff? Have you seen it Lofty?"

Just then, Lofty spotted the mice who were following Bob.

"Ooh arggghhh!" squealed Lofty. **"MICE!"**

"Mice?" asked Bob, confused. He turned around to look for the mice, but they ran behind him so he didn't see them.

Lofty was terrified, and sped off down the road toward the town.

"Come back Lofty," called Bob. "It isn't mice, it's only my boots."

Bob hurried off after Lofty, with the mice following behind his squeaky boots.

Lofty raced all the way to Bob's yard in a panic. Roley and Dizzy were there.

"Oh oh mice oh oh!" cried Lofty.

"Mice, Lofty? Where?" asked Dizzy.

Bob came running into the yard, with the mice still behind him.

"LOOK! M-MICE!" cried Lofty.

"Lofty, there aren't any mice, see?" said Bob.

He turned around to show Lofty, but this time he saw the mice.

"Ohh mice!" cried Bob, shocked. "Lofty, you were right!"

Bob walked around the yard and the mice followed close behind him.

"Ha ha. Look!" laughed Bob. "They like my squeaky boots, don't they?"

Just then, Bird arrived in Bob's yard and landed on Lofty. Spud came panting in behind him.

"Oh oh phew," sighed Spud. "Made it. All the way to Bob's Yard as the crow flies. Hee hee! Beat that, Bird!"

But Bird had already beaten him.

"Oh!" said Spud, disappointed. "Well, finally, I can have my cream puff."

He started to chomp happily on the cream puff and made such a mess that crumbs fell all over the ground. The mice ran over to eat them up.

"What have you got there, Spud?" asked Bob.

"Cream puff, Bob," mumbled Spud. "Er … oh … Is it yours?"

"Yes, it is mine," said Bob, annoyed. "You shouldn't take people's things without asking first."

"I didn't know Bob," said Spud. "I'm really sorry Bob."

The mice squeaked at Spud for more of his cream puff.

"Hey, get away, it's mine," cried Spud.

"Ha ha! Aren't you going to share it?" laughed Bob.

The mice chased Spud out of the yard, just as Wendy was coming in.

"Ha ha! Oh dear," said Wendy. "Where's Spud running off to?"

"Oh! … He's, he's just helping some friends get back home," laughed Bob.

"Bob, have you noticed?" said Wendy. "Your boots have stopped squeaking!"

"So they have," said Bob. "I must have broken them in with all that rushing around."

"You've had a busy day then?" asked Wendy. "Not really," replied Bob. "You could say it's been as quiet as a mouse!"

THE END!

Bob the Builder

Bob's Big Surprise

HINKLER BOOKS

Wendy was all packed and ready to visit her sister. Scoop was helping her by carrying her suitcase.

"Don't worry about us Wendy," said Bob. "You just enjoy your visit with your sister."

"Oh, I will. Oh my, she's got a lovely garden, with a patio and everything," sighed Wendy. "Unlike mine, which is a complete mess. All right, bye everyone! See you tomorrow night!"

"Goodbye!" cried the machines.

"I'll send Scoop to pick you up from the station!" called Bob.

"Ou-ww," frowned Dizzy. "I miss Wendy when she's not here."

"Don't worry Dizzy," said Bob. "We'll be too busy to miss her!"

"What do you mean Bob?" asked Dizzy.

"I've just had an idea," said Bob. "We're going to fix Wendy's garden up so it's as nice as her sister's!"

"Oh, good idea Bob," said Roley.

"We haven't got much time though," said Bob. "We'll have to start bright and early in the morning."

The next morning, the machines were ready for work.

"There won't be anyone in the office," Bob explained. "So I'll leave the answering machine on, and look in now and then to check the messages."

"Can we fix it?" called Scoop.

"Yes we can!" everyone shouted.

At Wendy's house, Bob surveyed the site.

"All right, let's see," he said. "We'll have a bit of lawn in the middle, a patio by the house, and over there, we'll put up a pergola."

"Ah ..." puzzled Lofty. "What's a pergola?"

"A big wooden frame thing," said Bob. "Very nice for sitting under."

"Can we have some flowers please? Wendy loves flowers!" asked Dizzy.

"Great idea Dizzy," said Bob. "We'll put a flower bed over there and I'll order some plants when I get back to the office later. All right everyone, let's get to it!"

Muck dug the flower bed, Lofty lifted the timber to build the pergola and Dizzy poured the cement for Wendy's new patio. Everything was going smoothly, so Bob decided to go back to the office to check his messages.

Meanwhile, back at the office, Bob was getting a lot of phone calls.

"Rrrring! Rrring!" went the phone.

"Hello, this is Bob's Building Yard," said Wendy's voice on the answering machine. "Please leave a message after the beep. **BEEEEP!!"**

"Waaaooohh!" squealed Pilchard. All the noise was disturbing her nap!

Soon the phone was ringing again.

"Rrring!! Rrring!!"

Pilchard was very annoyed. She flicked the telephone off the hook with her tail.

"Hello?" said a voice on the phone. "Is that Bob's Building Yard? Hello?"

Just then, Bob walked in the door.

"Oh my goodness!" he cried, picking up the phone. "Hello? Hello? Oh! Now how did that happen?"

Then Bob noticed the flashing light on the answering machine.

"Oh no! There's a load of messages too!" he said, and pushed a button on the machine.

The messages began to play, but then the tape got stuck.

Bob pressed a few more buttons to fix it, but the machine just made a bad scratching noise.

"Oh, oh!" cried Bob. "Why do I always have trouble with this answer machine? Where's that instruction book?" Bob scrabbled about the desk, looking under papers in a panic.

"Oh, never mind, I'll take care of it later," said Bob. "I must send this fax to the Garden Center." He faxed off the order, then noticed the time.

"Oh no! Nearly three o'clock!" cried Bob. "I'd better get back to Wendy's garden. See you later, Pilchard!"

Bob raced out the door, but the phone started ringing again. "Rrring, rrring!!"

"Waaarroohhh!" said Pilchard, annoyed. She hit the answering machine with her paw. The tape sped up and the machine started to chew it.

Soon there was tape everywhere.

Back at Wendy's house, the job was nearly finished.

"But, Bob, what about the flowers?" asked Dizzy.

"Oh, I've ordered them Dizzy," said Bob. "You and Muck can go and pick them up."

"Oh, good-ee!" cried Dizzy.

Bob started to pull up the last few weeds in the garden, but they were stubborn.

"Oh, I forgot my pitchfork!" said Bob. Bob had to go back to get it.

When he got back to the office, Pilchard was covered with tape from the answering machine and there was a cushion stuffed into the fax machine.

"Woah!" cried Bob. "Oh my goodness! What's happened here?"

"Meow ..." said Pilchard sweetly.

"It's no good looking all innocent Pilchard," said Bob. "When Wendy sees this, we'll both be in trouble! Now, how am I supposed to fix this? Oh! Too late! It's six o'clock. Wendy'll be back soon!"

He grabbed his pitchfork and raced out. When he got back to Wendy's house, Bob was in quite a state.

"Oh, come on everybody, we've got to get a move on!" he cried.

"Well, we're all done Bob," said Scoop. "There's just the pergola to finish off and the flowers to plant."

"Don't panic!" cried Bob. "I'm on the case! Scoop, you'd better go and meet Wendy ... go on!"

When Scoop got back with Wendy, there were loud noises coming from her garden.

"Goodness," said Wendy. "What on earth's that noise?"

"Oh that," said Scoop uncertainly. "Ah, that's just ... er ... a woodpecker!"

"If it is," giggled Wendy. "It's the biggest one in the world!"

Just then Bob appeared at the front door.

"Wendy!" cried Bob. "Close your eyes and come with me."

"What's going on?" laughed Wendy.

Bob led Wendy to the backyard.

"OK, you can open your eyes now!" cried Bob. "Surprise, surprise!"

75

Wendy opened her eyes and saw the beautiful new garden.

"Oh, Bob!" cried Wendy. "A patio! Oh, just right for barbecues. A pergola! I'll be able to sit outside on summer evenings. And a lovely flowerbed, with all of my favorite plants! Oh, thanks all of you!"

Wendy sat down on the patio and Bob brought her a tray of tea.

"Oh Bob, thank you," said Wendy.

"Well," said Bob guiltily. "Everything's in a bit of a mess. In fact, I was wondering if you could come in early and take care of it."

"Do you mean **Can I fix it?**" laughed Wendy. **"Yes, of course I can!"**

THE END

Bob the Builder

Pilchard Goes Fishing

HINKLER BOOKS

O ne morning, the machines heard some very strange noises coming from the house.

"Oh, you, you be still! Wooah! Heh heh! You're a slippery customer, aren't you?" they heard Bob say from inside.

Just then Wendy arrived. "Morning everyone!" she said. "Where's Bob?"

"He's in the house, Wendy," said Scoop.

"Talking to someone ..." said Muck uncertainly.

Inside, Wendy found Bob poking in the fish tank with a net. "Yup, come on," said Bob. Pilchard was watching with great interest.

"Oh. Where you going? ... Ah ... Oh!" said Bob.

"Bob?" giggled Wendy. "What are you doing?"

"Ohh! G'morning, Wendy," said Bob. "I thought it was about time I cleaned out Finn's tank. But he's not helping. Are you Finn?"

"No, I can see that," Wendy laughed. "You get going Bob. I'll take care of Finn."

"Thanks, Wendy," said Bob.

"See you later," said Wendy.

Pilchard was still watching Finn closely. "Miaooow!" she said.

In the yard, the machines were ready for work.

"Muck, I'll need you to help me; and Dizzy and Roley," said Bob.

"Can we fix it?" called Scoop.

"YES WE CAN!!!" everyone shouted.

Bob jumped on Muck and they headed out to fix some holes in the road.

"Er, shall I start mixing, Bob?" asked Dizzy when they arrived at the job.

"Yes, Dizzy. You do that … Oh no! I forgot the cement!" cried Bob. "Muck, would you go back to the yard and get a couple of bags for me please?"

"On my way Bob," said Muck.

"And hurry. We've got lots more to do today!" called Bob.

Meanwhile, Wendy put Finn in a bucket of water so she could clean his tank. Suddenly, she heard a loud crash in the yard and rushed outside with the bucket. Muck had come roaring into the yard and swerved to avoid Bird, crashing into the post of the car port.

"Oh," cried Wendy. "Are you all right, Muck?"

"I'm OK. Oh, I'm really sorry, Wendy," said Muck miserably. "Bob sent me back for some cement and he said to hurry and I did but I hurried a bit too fast and … you won't tell him, will you?"

"Oh Muck. Bob'll understand," soothed Wendy.

Wendy put Finn's bucket down and went to inspect the broken post.

"This shouldn't be too hard to fix," said Wendy. "Now, we'll have to dig this out and we'll need to set a new support in cement."

"Cement! That's what I came for!" said Muck.

Wendy put three bags of cement into Muck's tipper. While she was busy, Pilchard snuck over to peek into Finn's bucket.

"See you later, Wendy. And thanks!" called Muck, heading back.

At the site, Dizzy mixed and poured the cement that Muck brought and Roley started rolling it flat.

Bob's cell phone rang. "Hello, Bob the Builder. Oh hi, Wendy," said Bob as he answered it. "Yes, course you can. Bye bye." Bob clipped his phone back on his tool belt. "Dizzy? Could you go back and help Wendy? She needs to have some cement mixed."

"Goody!" cried Dizzy.

"I wonder what Wendy wants cement for?" mused Bob.

Muck groaned, feeling very guilty.

90

At the yard, Pilchard was still watching Finn closely, while Wendy and Lofty were busy fixing the shelter.

"All right Lofty," said Wendy. "I just want you to pull the old support out of the ground."

"Oh. Er … yeah … I think I can do that," said Lofty, as he began to pull hard on the stump.

"I can lift it … ah … I can lift it!" Lofty muttered, straining.

While Lofty worked, Pilchard took her chance to slide a paw into Finn's bucket.

Suddenly, Lofty freed the stump from the ground with a mighty tug that sent it flying toward Pilchard.

"Miaooow!" squealed Pilchard as she jumped quickly out of the way.

"Ohh, right!" said Wendy. "While we're waiting for Dizzy, I think I'll make some iced tea."

As soon as Wendy went inside, Pilchard crept back over to the bucket.

"Miaow …" said Pilchard, as she looked in.

Just then, Dizzy arrived back in the yard.

"Hi Wendy! I'm home!" shouted Dizzy.

Pilchard was surprised and leapt away.

"Oh my! What happened?" said Dizzy when she saw the damaged shelter.

"Oh, just a little accident," said Wendy, coming out of the house. "But now that you're here Dizzy, you can help us. We need some cement in this hole to hold the new support."

"Oh goody!" grinned Dizzy. "I've got lots left." She began to mix.

"There," said Wendy, as they put the post in place. "Now, we just need to screw the roof back down to the new support and wait for the cement to set."

Wendy climbed a ladder to screw in the new post and was just finishing when Bob and the others arrived back in the yard.

Muck was very relieved that Bob wouldn't find out about the accident. "Fantastic! Oh Wendy, you've done a great j–" Muck stopped.

"A great what?" asked Bob. "Muck? What's going on?"

"Oh … I had a little accident, Bob," said Muck uneasily. "I skidded to miss Bird and smashed into the car port … Sorry Bob."

"There's no need to be sorry," said Bob. "You didn't do it on purpose. And Bird's fine."

"Toot, toot, toot!" said Bird in agreement.

"And Wendy, our excellent builder, has fixed it!" said Bob.

While they talked, Pilchard crept back to Finn's bucket and licked her lips. This time she was sure she'd catch Finn.

"Toot, toot, TOOT!!" cried Bird, to warn the others.

"Wrrrrooowiaow!!!" said Pilchard angrily.

"Oh Pilchard! Bird!" cried Wendy. "I totally forgot poor Finn! With all the excitement with the accident and everything, I forgot I was cleaning out the fish tank. But Pilchard and Bird have just reminded me!"

98

Wendy and Bob went inside to finish the clean-up.

"There you go, Finn. Now your tank's nice and clean, thanks to Wendy," said Bob, as he popped Finn back into his sparkling tank.

Pilchard flicked her tail in annoyance. She knew she had missed her chance to go fishing.

"Pilchard?" called Wendy. "You've been such a clever cat, you deserve a special treat, don't you? Would you like some fresh fish?"

But Pilchard had had quite enough fish for one day. "Wrroaww" she sighed, as she collapsed on the floor.

The End

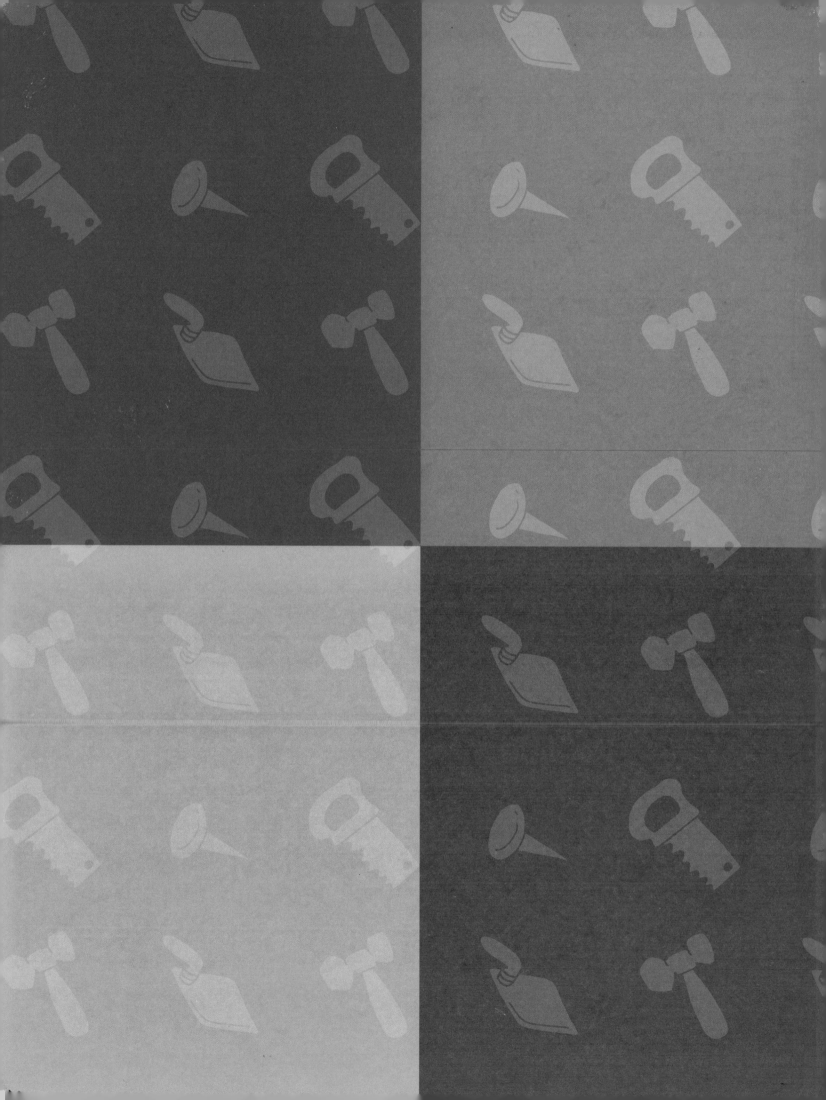